For Antek – Love, Mummy xxx

First Edition 2018
Kane Miller, A Division of EDC Publishing

Text and illustrations copyright © Emilia Zebrowska, 2018

For information contact:
Kane Miller, A Division of EDC Publishing
www.kanemiller.com
www.edcpub.com
www.usbornebooksandmore.com

Library of Congress Control Number: 2017963611

Manufactured by Regent Publishing Services, Hong Kong
Printed July 2018 in ShenZhen, Guangdong, China
1 2 3 4 5 6 7 8 9 10

ISBN: 978-1-61067-783-7

Fox's Box

Emilia Zebrowska

Kane Miller
A DIVISION OF EDC PUBLISHING

"What's in that box?"
asked the **curious** fox.

"It's really big!"
said the **nervous** pig.

"Bigger than my house,"
said the **scared** mouse.

"It could be a chair,"
said the **grumpy** bear.

"Don't make me laugh," said the **rude** giraffe.

"I'm sure it's a clock,"
said the **proud** peacock.

"Don't push your luck,"
said the **cheerful** duck.

"I hope it's a log,"
said the greedy frog.

"It's so your style,"
said the jolly crocodile.

"Maybe it's honey," said the hopeful bunny.

"Let's open the box!"
said the **excited** fox.

"It's a cake!"
said the **delighted** snake.